Snoopy for President!

By Charles M. Schulz

Adapted by Maggie Testa

Illustrated by Scott Jeralds

SIMON SPOTLIGHT

New York   London   Toronto   Sydney   New Delhi

SIMON SPOTLIGHT
An imprint of Simon & Schuster Children's Publishing Division
1230 Avenue of the Americas, New York, New York 10020
This Simon Spotlight paperback edition July 2016
© 2016 Peanuts Worldwide LLC
SIMON SPOTLIGHT and colophon are registered trademarks of Simon & Schuster, Inc.
For information about special discounts for bulk purchases, please contact
Simon & Schuster Special Sales at 1-866-506-1949 or business@simonandschuster.com.
Manufactured in the United States of America 0816 LAK
10 9 8 7 6 5 4 3 2
ISBN 978-1-4814-6648-6
ISBN 978-1-4814-6649-3 (eBook)

It's a beautiful, sunny afternoon, and Snoopy is doing what he loves best—daydreaming on top of his doghouse. But then he hears something down below. It's Woodstock and the other birds hopping by, holding signs for different candidates for class president.

I had forgotten that this was an election year, thinks Snoopy.

One person who hasn't forgotten is Lucy. She wants her little brother Linus to become the next class president.

"But I could never be class president," says Linus. "Think of the work. Think of the responsibility."

"Think of the power," Lucy adds.

Linus smiles. Actually, that sounds pretty good. "I'll do it!" he shouts.

At school the next day Linus doesn't waste any time getting the word out.

"If I am elected class president, I will demand immediate improvements," he announces. "Any little dog who happens to wander onto the playground will *not* be chased away, but will be welcomed with open arms!"

Snoopy likes the sound of that!

But Linus has some competition. Pigpen is also running for class president, and some students are planning to vote for him. Lucy takes it upon herself to convince everyone in the school to vote for Linus.

"Hey, you!" she shouts on the playground. "Who are you gonna vote for?"

"Uh, Linus, for sure," the kid replies.
"Well, you better!" says Lucy. She
turns to Linus. "According to my
private poll, you now have eighty-five
percent of the vote."

The next day Violet approaches Linus. She's a reporter for the school paper. "Would you care to tell us what you intend to do if you're elected class president?" she asks.

"I intend to straighten things out!" Linus says passionately. "We are in the midst of a moral decline! We are—"

Violet interrupts him. "I'll just put down that you're very honored and will do your best if elected."

"The press is against me," whines Linus as Violet walks away.

But Linus isn't done with the press. Schroeder wants to take photographs of him and Pigpen for the school paper. "Let's pose you both with a dog," explains Schroeder. Snoopy comes bounding out and steals the spotlight. "Looking good, Snoopy," says Schroeder. "Maybe *you* should run for class president."

Snoopy likes the sound of that!

That afternoon Snoopy transforms his doghouse into campaign headquarters. Woodstock will be his campaign manager. He's got a lot of ideas about what Snoopy should do, but he gets so excited by them that he paces right off the doghouse!

My campaign manager isn't too bright, thinks Snoopy.

Snoopy will just have to campaign by himself. He goes to school the next day and holds up a big sign with a paw print on it.

Lucy is not pleased. "I wouldn't vote for you if you were the last beagle on earth!" she tells him.

Snoopy starts to cry.

"All right," Lucy gives in. "If you were the last beagle on earth, I'd vote for you."
When Lucy walks away, Snoopy smiles.

Sally approaches Snoopy next. "I'm not sure if I'll vote for you or not," she says.

Once again Snoopy starts to cry.

"All right! All right!" Sally says. "I'll vote for you. Just stop crying!"

He's got a winning campaign strategy!

When Violet comes by, she asks Snoopy why she should vote for him.

"I mean, can you give me a reason?" she asks.

When Snoopy doesn't answer, she just walks away.

But Snoopy does know the answer. *For one thing, I'm kind of groovy!* he thinks.

Not much later Lucy comes by again.

"I think you're going about this all wrong," she tells Snoopy. "You've got to do more than just carry a sign. If you're going to get elected, you're going to have to shake a lot of hands and kiss babies."

Snoopy does *not* like the sound of that!

That evening Snoopy climbs back on top of his doghouse. Tomorrow is Election Day. Each candidate for class president will give one final speech before the students vote. What will Snoopy say in his speech?

I'll tell my latest anti-cat joke, he thinks. *The dog audience will love it. But wait . . . are there any dogs at the school aside from me?*

At the assembly the next morning, Pigpen makes his speech first.

"If I'm elected class president," Pigpen begins, "I promise to—"

"You can't be class president, Pigpen," Violet yells from the audience. "You're a mess, and you have no dignity."

But Pigpen isn't discouraged. He reaches down, picks up a top hat, and puts it on. He looks just like a dusty Abe Lincoln! Very presidential, Pigpen!

Linus goes up to the podium next. In the audience Lucy smiles. There's no way Linus can lose as long as he sticks to the script she wrote.

Linus clears his throat. "I want to talk to you this morning about the Great Pumpkin," he begins.

Everyone in the audience starts to laugh.

"AUGH!" Lucy screams.

The Great Pumpkin was the one thing Linus *wasn't* supposed to talk about. His chances of winning are over!

Snoopy is the final candidate to take the stage. Before he goes on, Schroeder asks Snoopy what he plans to say.

"Woof!" Snoopy replies.

"He's done for," Schroeder says to Linus.

But Snoopy is determined. He walks proudly to the podium, clears his throat, and lets out a confident bark. "Woof!"

The crowd goes wild.

A few hours later the votes are tallied. . . .

And Snoopy wins the election!

Linus and Pigpen are disappointed.

"I'm sorry you didn't get elected class president, Pigpen," says Linus.

"You too," says Pigpen. "Here we thought having photographs with a dog would get *us* votes, but instead, they all voted for the dog!"